Deng, Nyan-Nhialdit and the Talking Crow

Kuir ë Garang

The Nile Press
Calgary, Alberta

First Edition 2013

Illustrations by *Nhial Korow*

ISBN: 978-0-9916789-5-2

PUBLISHED BY THE NILE PRESS
http://thenilepress.com
Calgary
Printed in USA

† For JRS Sisters †

Contents

Chapter One

Deng, his Sister and his Friends

Deng sighed looking at his mum.

"It's not that I don't like playing with her. It's just that when it's raining, my friends and I really get to have a good time."

Deng said standing on the hut's threshold. His young sister, Nyankor, stared lovingly at him.

Not now you lovely little thing. Deng stared at Nyankor with understandable ambivalence.

"She's also your friend you know."

"I know that mama."

Deng Akoy was a slim, nine-year old boy, who loved to play with his friends. He lived with his mum, Atong, his dad Akoy, and his baby sister, Nyankor. To his good fortune, Deng's compound faced a thick, ominous forest. During rainy seasons, Deng and his friends loved playing in the forest. There was one big mango tree Deng and his friends always played under when it wasn't raining. Their joy in the rain was immeasurable.

Deng loved his friends dearly so they played in the rain every Friday after school. Saturday was their most important day when they'd play hide and seek in the bushes or discuss friendship stuff. At times their conversations were silly.

Sometimes they discussed school issues or good manners.

Deng's lovely and beautiful friends were three girls and two boys. The girls were Nyoka, Nyakong and Aluel. The boys were Lado and Ochang. They all shared the same sentiment: best friends forever.

"Where are you going, Deng? Try to play with your sister this time," his mum requested.

"I'm going to play with my friends, mama," Deng said, his eyes pleading.

He'd started to walk away, towards the forest.

"How about your baby sister, Deng?" his mum asked again.

Deng suddenly stopped. He raised his hands and slapped them onto his laps. From the look on his face, he was annoyed.

"Mama, it's raining!"

"Okay. Go have fun, but remember

your sister next time."

Deng smiled, raised his hands in excitement and sprinted away.

His face lit with both appreciation a- nd anticipation. Ne- ar their play-ground was an old lady named old Nyan-nhial or Nyan-nhialdit. She was so old and wrinkled-faced that Deng thought she was born at the beginning of the world. Her husband, Jada, was equally old. They'd smile at Deng anytime he passed by their home. Jada was from a tribe in South Sudan called Bari and Nyan- nhialdit was from another tribe called Jieng or Dinka. Nyan-nhialdit once called Deng on his way to his friends and asked him to fetch her water from her cold-water pot. The pot is called *ziir* in Arabic. When Deng had brought her the water, she strangely told him to sit.

Nyan-nhialdit told Deng that tribes are just like names and colors. She advised Deng to be friends with any girl she liked as long as she was of good character. At first Deng didn't know what tribe meant. He didn't know his friends were all from different tribes. When Deng's mum, Atong, affirmed what Nyan-nhialdit had said, she became his favorite old lady. He started to value her opinions.

"Love can be stupid sometimes. However, it defies what people have come to see as unbreakable borders between tribes," the old lady had said.

Deng found his friends playing in the open space near their favorite mango tree. Nyoka and Aluel were holding the jumping rope. Nyakong was jumping in and out of the loop. Ochang and Lado were throwing maize cobs at themselves.

"Look, Deng is coming!" shouted Nyoka excitedly.

"He's running like a gazelle," Nyakong said laughing shyly.

The boys suddenly stopped running around when they saw Deng.

"Why're you running like someone is chasing after you?" Lado asked and threw a cob at Ochang.

"I'm competing with the rain," Deng said heaving heavily.

The boys and girls all laughed excitedly at once.

"The last time I checked from your mother, your name means *rain*," said Ochang.

"You look really funny. But why do you want to compete with the rain?" asked Lado.

Deng raised his right hand to shush Lado. He was still breathing heavily.

"It's because the rain is beautiful. That's why," said Nyoka raising her voice.

"What would happen if we didn't have rain?" Deng asked.

"People would die," Ochang said.

"No, people wouldn't die. There's a river," Deng explained. "We can still get water from the river."

"You know the water in the river comes from the rain."

"But why are we talking about that?" asked Aluel with a frown. She was both curious and disturbed by Deng's question. They all stared curiously at Deng.

"Because we're friends and friends discuss stuff," Ochang said.

"But why did you ask in the first place?" asked Lado. Lado loved asking questions but he didn't like answering them.

Deng remembered one time when their English teacher, Madam Puru, had asked Lado to be quiet. Lado had asked about why people can't see wind. All the students in class laughed. Madam Puru didn't laugh. When she asked Lado to say what he thought, he ended up asking another question.

Deng shook his head and looked at his friends.

"I was wondering about our friendship," said Deng.

"What about our friendship?" Lado asked.

Ochang laughed loudly and tapped Deng on the back of his head.

"Why did you do that?" Deng asked.

"Yes, that laugh is not nice," said Nyakong

"Deng thinks we're friends because of the rain," Lado said laughing and singing mockingly looking at Deng.

"But we're happy when we play in the rain," Deng said.

"Why are you asking only this time?" asked Aluel.

Deng cupped his hands to tap rain water. He then looked at Aluel.

"I feel happy when I think of the six of us playing in the rain," Deng said and looked down.

"We all feel the same," Nyakong said quietly.

The friends realized the strange expression on Deng's face.

"You don't look fine, Deng. Is anything wrong?" asked Nyakong.

Having seen the concern on his friends' faces, he poured the water onto the ground and looked at them one by one.

"I don't know..."

"Come on!" urged Nyoka.

"Every single day mum wants me to play with my sister."

"What's wrong with that?"

"When it's raining!"

"Oh! That's why you were asking that question," remarked Ochang.

"Do you love her?" Lado asked.

"That's not a good question," Nyakong said looking disapprovingly at Lado.

"Why are you guys always this serious? Have a sense of humor."

Lado said a little upset.

"Don't feel bad, Lado," said Nyakong.

"No, you guys are always going against what I say."

"There are some issues that are not good to joke about," Ochang said and started to walk towards the village. The rain had stopped. Deng followed and the rest did the same.

"Of course I love her. It's just that I feel good playing with you all in the rain," explained Deng.

"I'm sorry!" said Lado.

"We know why you said what you said, Lado," Nyoka said and ran ahead of the rest.

"I love when she does that," Aluel marvelled, looking lovingly at Nyoka.

"Who wouldn't love Nyoka in this world?" Ochang said delightfully.

"I wouldn't!" Lado said, tapped Nyoka on the back and ran ahead. He's such a boy, Nyoka thought and ran after Lado.

"I'll catch up with you in a second. Don't bother running," Nyoka said.

"You know that Jamaican guy who runs like wind?"

Lado said running away from the rest.

"Husain Bolt?" said Ochang.

"You wish!" Nyoka mocked.

"You can't even beat Nyankor," said Nakong with a smile.

"No! That's not fair!" Aluel said.

Lado suddenly stopped as Nyoka slipped on the wet grass and fell on her buttocks. They all laughed excitedly.

Nyoka turned, still on the ground.

"Talk to your mum about Nyankor," said Nyoka, staring at Deng.

Nyoka loved talking with a raised voice. Her chit-chats were always a delight to the group. She was like the comic of the group. Her absence was easy for the group to feel.

The thunder rumbled and they all cringed.

"I feel like I hate her sometimes," Deng said of her sister.

"Do you talk to your mum seriously about Nyankor?" Lado asked.

"I do."

"Then?"

"When I insist, she let me go."

"Then what's the problem?"

"The guilt," Nyakong said quietly.

"How does guilt come in here?" Aluel asked.

"He feels like he's letting his sister down by leaving her at home," Ochang said.

Lado ran ahead, turned and faced the rest as he walked backwards. His face was shining with a lingering question. He smiled sheepishly and said: "So he left us then for her?"

"Again, Lado, that's not a fair question!" Aluel said.

"Why can't you guys just call me Mr. Unfair?" Lado said, still walking backwards.

"Because you're sweet most of the time," Nyoka shouted.

"But you know I'm with her all the time," Deng complained.

The six friends walked slowly to the village. It was getting dark. As the rumbling of thunder and the flickering of lightening slowed down, they were near the village.

Deng imagined what he would do without his friends. *I'm stupid thinking about that.*

Nyoka was a short, ten-year old with a brown, oval face. She loved being loud and making her friends laugh. Her hair was always braided in what they called *Kura* in Arabic. Changing their conversation to jovial mood was her specialty. *Nyoka the good parrot*, Aluel always sang.

Aluel was a slender nine-year old, who was the most curious among them. Her face was narrow and dark. She was the one who always wanted to know why things happen. *Ms. Einstein*, as Lado always said. Mr. Majok, their science teacher, had shown them a funny looking man with a wild, white hair and a smoking pipe.

Mr. Majok had told them that Mr. Einstein was the smartest man to ever live. He told them that Einstein's people were persecuted in Germany just like South Sudanese were in Sudan. You could be that smart if you study hard, he'd told them.

But did they gather all the men in the world to determine that he was the smartest, the students had asked. Mr. Majok had laughed, very much amused by the kids' apt curiosity.

Lado was ten and annoying in a way his friends liked. He was short and very thin. His words were meant to get people stirred up. He didn't like giving answers to questions. His only delight was to make fun of his friends' answers. Ochang called him, *the destroyer*.

Ochang was the John Garang of the group, as Nyakong always said. He had answers for all his friends' questions. During times of difficult debates, he was the one who always restored order. He was the oldest in the group, at eleven. His face was dark and plain. There was a birth mark on his left cheek. God put it there, he always said.

Nyakong was the quietest among them. While Ochang provided leadership, Nyakong was the one who always cautioned Lado against any mischievous tricks.

"Talk to your mum about Nyankor," Nyoka shouted as the friends parted.

"And tell your mum we need *Awal wala* next weekend." Lado said running away.

"And tell your mum we need *asida* and *mula khudhura* the following weekend," Deng said laughing and ran home.

Chapter Two

Deng Hates the Rain

*D*eng was happy it didn't rain the previous weekend. He couldn't have gone to the playground with his friends. His mum had gone to Kaya market to buy sesame and *mandesha*. Oil and flour were also running out in the house.

Thank you rain! You're very nice!

However, the Saturday after, things weren't looking good for Deng. *She's going to the market again?*

There was no way Deng liked the idea. He'd heard his mum discussing going back to the market with their neighbor, Nyambura.

16

Nyambura was a lady from a neighboring country, Kenya. She was married to Deng's neighbor. Their neighbor was a man from a tribe called Murle.

Deng hated talking about tribes because of Nyan-nhialdit's caution. *I hate that too old Nyan-nhialdit.*

But Deng's mum always talked about so and so is from this and that tribe. He's from this and that ethnic group. Balancing issues was becoming important to Deng as a result.

Since Nyambura started going to the market with Deng's mum, his agony began. The sight of Nyambura meant missed good times. A contorted face and growling stomach were becoming signs of Nyambura's presence. *Rain, please don't fall today.*

Deng was playing with Nyankor next to the goat's shed. Nyankor was playing with a wooden cart used for helping kids walk. Her toys were scattered all over the front side of the hut. The sky was showing signs of potential rain.

"Push it! You can't be that weak," Deng said frowning at his little sister.

"She's just two, Deng."

Startled, Deng suddenly turned only to see Nyambura staring at him. Embarrassed by his action, Deng smiled shyly.

"We're just playing."

"Your vocal tone didn't sound like you were playing."

Go away you're my trouble!

"We were playing," Deng stood his ground.

Stop talking you're my trouble!

"Just remember that. Is your mum inside?"

God don't let them go today! Please God!

"Yes, she's inside."

"I'll bring you something nice from the market today."

Oh no, Oh no!

"I don't...I mean, thank you."

Deng looked away with profound bitterness. He tried to frown but Nyambura looked back with a smile so Deng forced one big, mechanical smile. After Nyambura had entered the hut,

Deng looked at the sky. There were some nimbus clouds in the sky. Mr. Majok had told them that

Nimbus clouds hang really low and are the cause of rain most of the time. *Be a good boy please. Go away! Go!*

Nyankor curiously looked at Deng.

"No, no...I'm not talking to you. I'm talking to the clouds."

"How can you talk to the clouds?" Nyambura asked as Deng turned.

I don't like you.

"Well, I don't want it to rain."

"Why?"

"Because I'm playing with my sister."

"Oh...that's sweet!"

Oh, that's sweet! Leave my mum alone. Deng mentally mimicked Nyambura's voice. If it rained, his good time with friends wouldn't happen. *Nyambura?*

But Deng remembered the grumpy voice of old Nyan-nhial giving warning.

"When I tell you something you don't agree with, don't chide me internally. Let me know," the old lady had said.

Deng had smiled because what Nyan-nhialdit was explaining was something he didn't agree with.

The old lady was explaining to Deng the value of turning the other cheek.

"Kids in school would call me a sissy," Deng had complained.

"It's better to be a sissy and safe than to be a brave fool and unsafe."

"But how do you benefit if you turn the other cheek?"

"How do you benefit if you fight?"

"My friends and others would respect me."

"Only if you win!"

"But they'd know I tried."

"So you mean to say you actually don't have a goal in doing that?"

"We're kids. We don't have goals."

"That sounds stupid, Deng, don't you think?"

"No!"

"So you come here to waste my time?"

Deng knew his words didn't come out right.

"I'm sorry!" he said remorsefully.

"Are you apologising to me? I'm old. Everything we're saying here is about you, not me."

"Oh!"

Deng turned to see Nyambura waving at Nyankor.

"We'll be back soon," Atong said as she came out of the hut. Nyambura was ready with her bag.

"Okay, mama,"

No, Nyambura!

As Atong and Nyambura left, Deng stared pleadingly at the sky. *I'll hate you if you rain.*

Deng prayed for the rain not to rain. But then Nyankor started crying. Deng ran into one of the huts called *malbak* or kitchen, where food items were kept. He grabbed a bottle of milk and two bananas. Nyankor smiled when she saw Deng with milk and banana.

"You like them, eh?"

Nyankor started laughing and ran towards Deng. But as Deng handed the banana to the delighted Nyakor, the rumble of the thunder arrived together with the first drops of rain.

"You..."

Deng's friends came running towards Deng's family homestead. They were joyous as they were starting to enjoy the rain.

"Deng, take Nyankor to your mum!" Nyoka shouted.

Completely angry given the situation, Deng remained quiet and pulled his sister towards the hut.

"Oh, Deng is scared of the rain!" Lado said running toward the hut as Deng entered.

"I think something is wrong with him," Nyakong said and walked towards the hut.

"He's just playing with us."

"Deng?" Ochang called.

Deng remained silent and indifferent.

"I think something is wrong with him," Aluel said.

"He's finally chosen Nyankor over us."

"Stop that please!" Nyakong warned Lado.

Nyakong quickened her steps and entered the hut. She stared at Deng as he sat gloomily on the *bambar* (stool). Nyakor was busy eating her banana.

"Are you ok? We called you but you didn't respond to us!" Nyakong said with concern in her voice.

"I can't go with you."

"Why?" Nyakong said with a frown.

Deng silently stared at Nyakong then pointed at Nyankor.

"Oh, your mum isn't here."

Deng nodded as Nyakor laughed and threw her banana at Nyakong.

"I'm sorry!" Nyakong said.

"Me too."

"Don't feel bad. You're doing something good for your sister."

"Why does this happen to me and why now?"

Nyakong walked slowly and crouched next to Nyankor. "There's always a next time."

Deng angrily looked down. Nyankor was pulling excitedly at her brother's toes. Amused by the little girl's playfulness, Nyakong stared at Nyankor and laughed.

"Don't worry, it'll still rain," Nyakong assured.

"I hate rain, I hate Nyambura..."

"Hey, don't say that! It's only today. You don't know who's listening."

"I don't care who's listening."

"Be nice. It's only today, ok?"

"Go and enjoy your time!" Deng said with apparent resignation.

Nyakong waved at the siblings and left the hut.

"What's wrong with him?" Lado asked as Nyakong emerged from the hut. She first sighed, looked at Ochang and Aluel and said.

"He can't come."

"Why?" Aluel asked with a deep frown.

"He's ditched us for his sister. I told you."

"Stop this one now, Lado!"

"But I'm right, right?"

"Whatever Lado! His mum has gone to the market," Nyakong said with resignation.

"So he's taking care of his sister," Ochang said.

"Let's go then," Nyoka said and ran towards the forest.

Deng slowly walked to the door as his friends playfully ran to the playground. They were happy. He wasn't.

"I hate you rain. I don't care whether you fall again or not. Just go. Last Saturday you listened to me but now you don't want to listen. I'm helping my sister, can't you understand that? What sort of a *thing* are you anyway?"

Chapter Three

The Rain is Angry

*T*hree weeks passed by without any drop of rain. *When I'm free, you refuse to come.* Deng was scanning the sky like an ancient rainmaker. Madam Puru had explained to them the ancient wisdom of rainmakers. But Madam Puru had told them that rainmakers had to appease the Gods to make up for the anger the Gods had towards the people in the village who'd done bad deeds.

Who in this village has done something bad?

Deng hoped to see any sign of nimbus clouds. He could only see some feather-like cirrus clouds. They were really high up in the sky.

Burdened and worried, Deng looked at their playground mango tree. It was almost drying out. A few birds perched on the tree stared at him. They looked angry. *I didn't do anything, you guys!*

The birds then flew down directly towards Deng. He ducked. They missed his head by inches. Deng had thrown himself onto the ground to avoid being hit. Confused, he stared at the crows. They were now high up in the sky.

"That was weird."

Deng then shot up, dusted himself and ran to Nyan-nhialdit's house.

Yaba Jada was sitting outside on his plastic chair.

He was singing softly in Bari.

"She's inside," he said before Deng could even ask.

"Thank you *Yaba*," Deng said.

He dashed to the hut; his face flooding with sweat.

"Are you coming here to talk about the drought?"

Deng frowned: "How did you know?"

"That's the main topic these days, isn't it?"

Deng sat down slowly on the mat spread on the floor. He then reflectively stared on the ground. Nyan-nhialdit was arranging beads on a thread. The beads were beautiful and in different colours.

"Does it always happen this way?"

"Yes, it has a couple of times. It was not like this though," she said.

She was twitching her mouth, looking keenly at the beads. Having realized Deng's curiosity, she smiled. She then glanced occasionally at Deng.

Deng looked up. "What's the difference?"

Nyan-nhialdit stopped piling the beads onto the thread. "Someone has annoyed the Rain-God. He's someone who shouldn't have."

Deng grimaced. "How do you know that?"

"Can you even ask that question now?"

"I'm sorry!"

Deng shot up, looked at Nyan-nhialdit and wondered: "I thought you didn't believe the rain-makers story."

She frowned and turned her *bambar*. "Truth is not believed it's known!"

And what's that supposed to mean? Deng looked outside then looked back at Nyan-nhialdit.

"How do we end it?"

She glanced at Deng and resumed her beads arrangement. "Find out the culprit."

"How?"

"I don't know."

"How do you suppose we do it?"

"Ask the rain-makers."

Nyan-nhialdit was struck by Deng's curiosity. She stopped arranging her beads, again. With a smile she said: "You seem to be interested in this."

Deng frowned. "It's really dry and hot out there."

The old lady laughed. She pulled her bambar toward Deng. Her orange gum made her face look funny. "Is that all? I was born when you were not even a concept. You can't hide things from old people, you know."

"I don't know...mm...we like playing in the rain."

"Don't worry. The rain will come."

"I know but when?"

"I'm not a rain-maker."

Deng walked back towards Nyan-nhialdit. "How do we find out the person who's annoyed the Rain-God?"

"Ask your mum."

"She'd think I'm crazy."

"And you think I wouldn't?"

"Would you?"

Nyan-nhialdit raised her eyebrows and angled her head to the right.

"You're wise and you know ancient stuff," Deng added.

He walked slowly back to the door. Nyan-nhialdit stared at him.

"I can help if you're honest with me."

"What do you mean?"

She smiled: "The Gods are watching and listening, you know."

"I don't know...but you'll think I'm crazy!"

"I thought you said..."

"This is different," Deng said interrupting old Nyan-nhial.

"I've lived for a long time. I'm approaching ninety years of age. I've seen and heard a lot."

Deng sighed hesitantly. "I don't know. Before I came here, a murder of crows flew right at me. It's as if they intended to harm me."

Nyan-nhialdit smiled and arched her eyebrows upwards.

"Go and find the rain-maker."

"Can you help me?"

"No!"

Nyan-nhialdit said and pulled her bambar away. She then resumed her beads arrangement.

"What's wrong?"

"I need to finish this before tonight."

Deng stared, completely taken aback. "Did I say anything wrong?"

"I said I need to finish this before night fall."

Surprised, Deng reluctantly walked to the door. He curiously looked back. Nyan-nhialdit sat indifferently and as busily as a bee. Confused, Deng shook his head and left. *What have I done?*

Not knowing what to do, Deng leisurely but dejectedly walked home. As he approached the mango tree, he found the same crows perched on it. *That's weird!* Very much curious, Deng peered at the crows. He then saw them fly away. Reminded of their previous action, he suddenly threw himself onto the ground. *Oh!* Embarrassed, he smiled to himself. *I'm such a coward.* The birds had not come his way. One of them was still perched on the tree though.

"These birds are so stupid!"

"I wouldn't say that if I were you."

Deng turned around 360 degrees. He could see no one. There was no one around so he looked up the tree. Perched proudly on the tree branch was only that rude crow. It was still staring sternly at Deng.

"Leave me alone!"

"I can't!"

Deng frowned, slanted his neck to the right and squinted at the crow. "I think I'm getting crazy. I can hear voices."

This is not good.

The crow then flew down the branch. Deng, like always, jumped to the ground.

"You're not crazy," the crow said.

"Are you the one talking? Noooooo!"

Deng sprang up, looked at the crow and sprinted away. He tripped on a tree stump and fell. Rattled and scared, Deng sprang up again and ran as fast as he could. The crow remained in the same spot, still staring at him. Deng looked back every now and then. The crow was still in the same place. A talking crow scared Deng more than he could imagine. The crow's size dwindled as he ran toward his home.

Chapter Four

The Talking Crow

*D*eng and his friends were saddened by the absence of rain. They sat gloomily under the mango tree. There was hardly any shade under the tree. The mirage in the distance turned village huts into thin films. Water-looking figures appeared at a distance. Dry leaves were all over their sitting area. It was searing hot.

"This is not good," Nyakong said.

Ochang got up and stared at the treetop. "I don't understand the drought sometimes."

"My grandma told me once that in the past, Gods used to stop the rain when angered," Nyoka said, sat up and started wiggling.

"How can they do that?" Lado asked.

"There used to be rain-makers who talked to the Gods."

"We still have them now," Aluel said.

"We can ask any elder in the village," Ochang said.

"I thought these things don't work anymore. We go to church you know."

"We'll have to talk to our parents," Nyakong said.

Deng was surprisingly silent. Looking tired and wearied, he sat there completely wordless.

"Deng!" Lado called out.

He still remained silent.

"Deng, are you ok?" Nyakong asked, surprise on her face.

"Oh, I'm ok!"

Aluel frowned and looked at him: "You look gloomy and tired."

"And you've been silent since we came here," Ochang said.

"What do you suppose we do?" Nyoka said loudly.

Deng still remained silent.

"Hey, man, you're freaking us out!"

"I don't know...I ..."

"We're your friends. What's wrong?" Nyakong asked.

He scanned his friends' faces slowly. They were staring expectantly at him.

"I remember you didn't want to come to the tree today," Ochang said.

Deng glanced toward Nyan-nhialdit's homestead and back at his friends. As he tried to look at the treetop, the same talking crow was looking at him. He quickly looked away.

"What's wrong?" Lado inquired.

"Let's go home!" Deng said raising his voice.

"Why?" Nyoka asked.

"Can we go to Nyan-nhialdit's home?" Ochang asked.

Deng suddenly sprang up. Still looking dejected, he said: "We have to go home."

"Did we wrong you?" Lado asked.

"No, it's not..."

Deng looked at the crow again. It was staring stubbornly at him.

"I'll wait until you talk to me."

"No, no!" Deng said, walked away slowly then sprinted away, fast.

All Deng's friends stared, completely taken aback. Then Nyoka and Aluel started running after Deng.

"Deng, wait!" Nyoka called.

"Please wait!" Aluel pleaded.

Nyakong, Lado and Ochang joined their friends. As they neared Nyan-nhialdit's homestead, Deng stopped. He swiftly glanced at the treetop near old Nyan-nhial's homestead. Like magic, the crow was staring at him, perched perfectly on a small branch.

"I'll wait until you talk to me."

"Oh God!" Deng said and started running again in full force. Nyoka and Aluel were like his tail. The rest were also running, a little behind. They continued running as Aluel and Nyoka kept shouting.

Deng! Please Stop! Please stop!

As they neared Deng's home, he stopped running. He looked back as Nyoka and Aluel came to a stop near him. They were panting like dogs on a hot day. Ochang, Lado and Nyakong joined them.

"What...was...tha-at?" Ochang asked still heaving from the sprint.

As Deng looked around, he spotted the crow near the pawpaw plants by their homestead.

Frightened to death, he tried to run to the hut. Nyoka caught him by the arm.

"What's going on?" Ochang asked.

"You're scaring us man!" Lado whined, his face shining with rare seriousness.

Not really sure about what to say, Deng ran into the hut. Confused and utterly dismayed, the friends stared at themselves.

"What's really going on?" Aluel said sorrowfully.

The friends decided to find out what was wrong with their friend. When they talked to Atong, she laughed and told them Deng was saying impossible things. He'd confided in his mum only to be laughed at. Atong implored Deng to talk to his friends. He refused. During the week, Deng avoided his friends. He refused to talk about his weird actions too.

Three days went by without any change in Deng's attitude and mood. On the fourth day Deng decided to go back to Nyan-nhialdit.

"What brings you here during the week?" she said.

Nyan-nhialdit was still not finished with her beads. She was still busy arranging them.

"I'm sorry I didn't tell you the truth last time."

She angled her head toward him. "I'm all ears."

He sighed, looked out of the door and back at her.

"I don't know. But please don't laugh at me."

She charmingly s- miled. "I've laughed long enough in my life. I'm not eager to laugh."

He sighed. "One of the crows that almost pushed me down is talking to me."

Nyan-nhialdit smiled, looked at Deng and said: "If you're talking to a crow then tell me what he's saying."

Deng frowned with resignation. "You don't believe me, do you?"

"You're skirting the problem."

"I'm sorry," he said. "I don't know. My mum always leaves me with my sister. I don't mind the rest of the days, but when it's raining, I get upset."

"Why?"

He sighed and moved his head around remorsefully.

"I love playing with my friends in the rain."

"So when you couldn't go and play, you were angry at the rain."

He nodded agreeably.

Nyan-nhialdit shrugged. "Then why are you coming to me?"

"What?" Deng asked with utter consternation.

"Yes. You refused to talk to the person with the message."

Deng frowned and shot up. *You're crazy old lady.*

"You call a crow a *person*? Do you know how crazy that sounds?"

"I'm not the one who said I talked to the crow."

You crossed the line old lady.

"So I'm crazy?"

"Did you hear me say that? I'm saying you're ignoring the messenger."

"You're..."

Deng suddenly stopped mid-sentence. His friends walked into the compound. They talked briefly with *Yaba Jada* and walked to the door of the hut.

"Come in!" Nyan-nhialdit called.

When Ochang spotted Deng, he suddenly turned and walked away.

"Where are you going?" Nyakong asked.

"Deng is in there?"

"So he ditched us for old Nyan-nhial?" Lado asked.

"Maybe he didn't ditch us. Maybe he's telling her something," Nyakong reasoned.

"We're his best friends. He should confide in us," Aluel said.

The friends walked away as Deng came out of the hut. He stared at them as they walked away, sad and dejected.

"Guys? Ochang? Lado?"

Deng tried to call his friends but they wouldn't budge. In school Deng tried to implore his friends but they remained adamant.

"To begin with, you refused to talk to us first. Then you confided in an old lady?" Ochang angrily said.

"First, you confided in your mum. Secondly, you confided in an old lady," Lado said.

"What's your age difference? Eighty?"

"You guys don't understand?"

"We can't understand what we don't know, can we, Deng?" Aluel curiously asked.

"I hope Nyan-nhialdit becomes your best friend. Let's go guys," Ochang said as they walked away. Nyoka and Nyakong walked away reluctantly. They stared at Deng with forgiving eyes. However, Boss Ochang had spoken. *Deng is done!*

Deng remained alone and rejected. *What have I done?* He stood outside the mud-walled and grass-roofed rectangular building that was their class. His friends, for the first time, walked away angry and disowning. He was alone. Tears dropped down his cheeks. He ran home feeling rejected. *I'm sorry! I'm sorry!*

Chapter Five

Angry Friends

A nother Saturday came with dread to Deng. *I'm all alone.* The village was still searing hot and dry. About the rain, Deng couldn't do much. However, he wanted to try to talk to his friends. They might forgive him. To make Deng's heart unsettled, they were all  sitting under their mango tree. It was unmercifully hot. As Deng neared the group, he realized Ochang wasn't in the group. They all looked down except Nyoka and Nyakong. The two girls were staring at Deng as he remorsefully walked towards them. They were all seated in a circle, facing the centre. Nyakong was the only one with her back turned to the group.

"Where's Ochang?" Deng asked.

"Did you miss your way?" Lado inquired.

Nyakong turned and looked admonishingly at Lado.

With his usual playfulness, Lado frowned at Nyakong. "What? I thought he was going to Nyan-nhialdit's homestead, his best friend!"

"We're all upset about this, but let it rest, would you?" Aluel said.

"Oh, I'm the bad guy and the one who ditched us is being protected!"

Deng walked slowly towards Lado. "You'll understand why I acted that way," Deng said and crouched. Lado squinted at Deng. "Yeah, the world has abandoned you."

"Stop it Lado, would you?" Nyakong said raising her voice for the first time. Lado got up angrily, trying to walk away. Before he could go far, he spotted Ochang walking towards them.

"I'll tell you guys everything. It'll sound funny, though," Deng said, still feeling lost and dejected.

Lado suddenly stopped and said with overt sarcasm: "We know you talk to crows."

"Yes!"

"What?" Nyoka said loudly.

"You mean to say your mum wasn't joking?"

Deng smiled. "No, she wasn't."

Lado came back slowly.

"How the hell are we supposed to believe that?"

Deng slowly sat down as Nyoka and Nyakong sat next to him in a circle. Ochang arrived and stared sternly at Deng. His face wasn't friendly and his voice was admonishingly dismissive.

"What're you doing here?"

"Please listen to him first," Nyakong requested.

"No, I can't! We come third in his consideration."

"Please listen to him!" Nyoka said and pulled Ochang's hand playfully.

"I've never lied to you guys and you know that," Deng said looking at his friends one by one. In all essence, he knew his friends' anger was warranted. It would have been a folly to blame them. However, he couldn't blame himself either. Anyone in his situation could have acted the way he did, at least.

"Then what happened? You ditched us for an old lady, man?" Lado said.

Deng slowly moved his eyes up the tree and looked at his friends again.

"You couldn't have believed me?" he said, his face becoming relaxed.

"And Nyan-nhialdit could?" Lado asked, still standing with unwavering indignation.

Deng was becoming surprisingly amused. He glanced at Ochang and stared at Lado. "Did you guys take it seriously when mum told you about the crow?"

"Hell no!" Ochang said.

"You see? That's why I was hesitant."

"But we're your friends. I doesn't matter what we think at first. We can talk it over."

"So you guys forgive me?"

Nyakong looked at Ochang and Lado, but they looked away. "Come on guys! He's our friend!"

Lado and Ochang still looked upset.

"Please forgive him!" Nyoka said.

"Come on guys!"

"I forgive him," Aluel said.

"O-kay!" Ochang said with difficulty.

Lado remained adamant.

"We have a problem to solve," Ochang said looking at Lado.

"Don't let this happen again," Lado said.

The girls all chorused: *yey!*

Chapter Six

*T*he friends were still confused.

"How are we supposed to go about talking to a crow?" Lado asked.

They were standing near old Nyan-nhial's homestead.

"I don't know. We have to talk to old Nyan-nhial," Deng said.

Deng and his friends made their way towards old Nyan-nhial's homestead. Yaba Jada was outside the house with their dog.

Solving Deng's claim was difficult for the kids. They knew people would think they were crazy.

Talking animals were issues they heard only in folk stories. They weren't real. However, Deng was so insistent that his friends had to give in. They only wanted to actually give him the benefit of the doubt. All of them knew that Deng would be the one to carry the blame cross should all become a folly.

"Are you kids still concerned about the rain?" Yaba Jada asked.

They all nodded without saying a word.

"Come on in, here. I'll tell you a story about rain."

Deng and his friends hesitated. They stood still not sure of what to say. Like always, Nyoka, excited by the mention of the rain story, ran towards Yaba Jada. Yaba Jada had a big, brown dog always by his side. Nyoka started grooming the dog then sat down. The rest followed her slowly and sat down around Yaba Jada.

"I know you guys came to see Nyan-nhial, but I'll steal her time."

The boys and girls readied themselves.

"In Jonglei state, there's a small clan called Adhiok. Don't ask me what Adhiok means because it is mythical and hard to understand. Adhiok is from Twi Dinka of Jonglei State. Their Payam headquarter is Wernyol. This clan calls itself a rain clan or Wun Man-Deng. They hated the rain before they made peace with it. The clan had ferocious warriors, who fought against other clans. They defied the British administration for a long time. Among the Twi Dinka clans and their neighbors, the Bor Dinka, they were the last to accept the British administration rule. They even fought the invading Turks. It's believed that this clan can fight anyone. They even once fought with the rain arguing that it kept on destroying their plans. Many Jieng people rely on cattle as a source of livelihood. They use dried cow dung as a source fuel. So every time they tried to spread moist cow dung (*weer*) in order to dry to be used for fuel, the rain started to rain. They got angry and fought with the rain. "

"How can someone fight rain? That sounds stupid!" Lado asked.

Having seen the changed expression on Deng's face, Yaba Jada stared at Deng.

"Yeah, that's my clan."

"Oh, that's why you like the rain! Cool!" Nyoka said.

"What's interesting is that they now worship the rain as a God," Yaba Jada continued.

"What happened when they fought the rain?" Lado asked.

"It didn't end well. The rain killed many of Adhiok people."

"Why do they still worship it then?" Nyakong asked.

"Maybe that's the God's will. You can't get away from the ways of the Gods. But the legend has it that some of their seers told Adhiok people that their action to fight the rain was wrong so they made peace with the rain. Now, I'm telling you this because someone has angered the rain. And I do believe it's someone from the rain clan."

Yaba Jada said and smiled. Everybody looked at Deng. Deng stared guiltily at Yaba Jada. While he was from Bari tribe, Yaba Jada knew almost all the mythical stories of all the major tribes in South Sudan. Deng didn't know how and why.

"Because I told you one mythical story about Deng's people, next time, I'll tell you about Nyoka's people, the Kakwa, and then all of you one by one. Now, do we know who annoyed the rain?"

"Yaba Jada, that's why we came here," Ochang said.

"I'm ready to apologize. I like playing with my friends in the rain. So when mum went to the market, with that Kenyan woman, and left me with my sister, I got really angry," Deng said remorsefully.

"He then cursed the rain," Ochang said.

"It becomes even worse when you're from the rain clan. Now, Nyan-nhial will tell you the rest."

"Is she from the rain clan?" Nyoka asked.

Yaba Jada smiled: "No, she's from Aweil in Northern Bhar Al Ghazal."

"How come you know so much about every tribe?" Aluel asked, looking bewildered.

"This is what it means to be a true South Sudanese. For you to consider South Sudan as your tribe, you have to prove it."

Deng and his friends got up. They'd been surprised by Yaba Jada in a way they couldn't imagine. They flocked, in a single line, into Nyan-nhialdit's hut. Nyan-nhialdit was putting final touches on her new cold water pot, the *ziir or töny* in Dinka. She'd just finished decorating her threaded beads.

"Why can't you kids leave me alone!" she said. She wasn't looking at them. Still looking at the pot in front of her, she pointed at the chairs behind her. The kids hesitated. Nyakong slowly walked to one of the chairs and sat down. The rest stood still.

"We need your help," Ochang said.

Nyan-nhialdit put the pot on its support, turned her stool and faced the kids. "I thought Deng knew how to get you help."

Deng slowly walked towards Nyan-nhialdit. "The crow hasn't come back again. We don't even know where to find it," he said.

"You've annoyed *him* again. You can't find him. It'll have to come to you."

"I don't want it...I mean, him, to find me alone."

Nyan-nhialdit looked sternly at Deng.

"You've annoyed a lot of people and you annoyed them by yourself. Or did you guys annoy the rain together?" she said looking at Deng's friends.

"Nooooo!" they all chorused.

"Ok! Go and find the crow."

"Please, Nyan-nhialdit, we need your help!" Nyakong said with pleading eyes. There was something enticingly calming about Nyakong's stare. Her stare was always innocent and reassuring.

"Please!" Nyoka said prayerfully, her hands clasped by her face.

"And how are we supposed to look for a crow?" Ochang asked.

Nyan-nhialdit scoffed: "That's your problem!"

"Please!" Nyoka said again.

Moved by Nyoka's lovely plea, Nyan-nhialdit stared lovingly at the pleading Nyoka. Nyakong was still staring pleadingly.

"Ok. There's an old man called *Umjalaba*. His house is about twenty minutes from here. Go and talk to him."

Deng frowned. "What are we supposed to tell him?"

"Okay, well, whatever you're looking for, I guess! Well, tell him Nyan-nhial sent us."

"Thank you so much

Nyan-nhialdit," Aluel said as they left.

Umjalaba's homestead was actually a full thirty minutes walking distance from Nyan-nhialdit's home.

The place was deep into the forest. There were a few dwelling places in that direction. The forest thickened as they walked on. Anxious to talk to the crow, the friends sprinted away. To their surprise, Umjalaba's place was only a lonely hut in the middle of the forest. The hut was dark from smoke. The sooty look of the hut was visible from the outside. The wall and the roof were all made from grass. There was no sign of life inside the house.

"This is weird!" Lado marvelled.

In front of the hut was a cluster of five banana plants. Near the banana plants was a long log that looked like a grinding motor. Near the hut's threshold was a grinding stone.

"This sure looks like a crow's home."

"That's not nice!" someone said behind them and they all jumped in fright. Umjalaba was a middle-age man. From his look, his age was between thirty-five and forty five years. He wore a multicolored sheet tied as a knot on this right shoulder. On his left land was an axe and on his right hand was a bundle of firewood. On Umjalaba's forehead was a line of spherical objects. They looked like large lined-up pimples.

"You're from Shilluk?" Deng asked with a frown.

Umjalaba walked towards his sooty hut and turned to the group. "Yes."

"But you don't look old!" Aluel wondered!

"Why am I supposed to be old?" Umjalaba asked.

"Only old people can do this," Nyoka said.

Umjalaba frowned at Nyoka: "Do what?"

"Never mind," Lado said.

"Aren't you supposed to be a woman?" Aluel asked.

"A *woman* is a definition or name. You're a girl because someone said someone who looks like you should be called a girl."

This is weird.

Aluel looked at her friends and shook her head repeatedly. "I don't understand."

Umjalaba turned towards the hut and threw the firewood down. He then turned to the group. "Is there a problem if I call these three boys, and these three girls?"

"Yeah!" they all chorused.

Umjalaba laughed.

"Does it change you?"

"No, it doesn't." Ochang said, bewildered by the thought that he could be called a girl.

"That's my point. Being called anything doesn't change you. You're who you are no matter what people say. Who you are can only change in your mind if you let people influence you."

This dude is weird, Lado thought.

"What brings you here?" Umjalaba asked walking towards his worn-out and sooty hut. He picked up one log of firewood and stood by the hut.

"Nyan-nhialdit sent us," Ochang said hesitantly.

"About what?"

"She said you'd know," Deng said.

"So you have no problem."

"We have."

"Then what's it?"

Deng looked disappointed. "We're looking for a crow who talks."

Umjalaba raised his eyebrows questioningly. "Ok?"

Ochang twitched his mouth, shook his head and walked towards Umjalaba. "My friend here said he talked to a crow."

Umjalaba entered his hut and called out. "Come on in!"

The friends stared curiously at themselves. They then entered uncertain of the condition inside. Inside, they were shocked at the cleanliness of the interior of the hut.

There were expensive suit cases, new wooden beds, chairs and a cassette player.

"Wow!" Nyoka said very much impressed.

"Who among you annoyed the Rain-God?"

They all stared curiously at Deng. Deng looked confused. *I said I'm sorry!*

Deng stared remorsefully at Umjalaba.

"I said stupid stuff about the rain. When the crow came to me, I got scared and ran away."

Umjalaba sat down on his bed. "So you want to talk to the crow."

Deng nodded. "Yes."

"And say what?"

"Listen to it...I mean...him."

"If he doesn't talk, what'd you tell him?"

Deng sighed. He was feeling tormented. "I don't know, apologize?"

"But the crow is only a messenger."

"I'll tell him to let the Rain-God know that I'm sorry."

Umjalaba stared at his curious visitors. They were all standing except Ochang and Nyakong, who were seated on two plastic chairs. The visitors remained silent as their host stared reflectively on the ground.

He then looked at them. "What have you learnt from this?"

"Not to curse?" Deng said.

Umjalaba shook his head. "No!"

"Crows can talk?" Lado said playfully.

Umjalaba frowned at Lado and pointed his right index finger at him.

"Family is important?" Aluel said.

Umjalaba smiled. "That's good but no."

"Let's respect animals and birds?" Nyoka said.

"It's not always good to think of yourself first all the time. There are times when putting others first is more important. Any time you're faced with a situation, ask yourself how any decision you make affects people around you."

Umjalaba's talk seemed aimless to Lado.

"How does this talk help us find the crow?"

"Do you guys need to talk to the crow or do you need the problem solved?"

None of the friends knew the answer.

"It'd be cool to talk to the crow," Lado said smiling.

"Shut up, Lado! We need the problem solved," Nyoka shouted.

"Okay, are we all agreed that the problem has to be solved?"

All said yes except Ochang. They all stared disapprovingly at Ochang as he sat staring at the stereo.

"Ochang?" Nyoka called.

"This sounds pointless," Ochang said.

"Are we agreed my friends?"

"Yes," Ochang said absent-mindedly.

"You can now go to Nyan-nhialdit. I'm done with you."

"What? She sent us here and you send us back to her?" Deng said raising his voice.

"Don't raise your voice. The forest is listening," Umjalaba said soothingly and quietly.

"This is not good," Lado said and walked out of the hut.

"Please, let us know how to get hold of the crow!" Deng pleaded.

"I said go to Nyan-nhialdit."

Deng angrily walked out of the hut as the rest stormed out.

Chapter Seven

The rain and the crow

*D*eng and his friends walked dejectedly towards their mango tree. They were getting tired, hungry and angry. The tree still looked leafless and withered. Confused and not knowing what to do, the group decided to sit under the tree. They were thinking of the next course of action.

"Let's go to Nyan-nhialdit's place," Nyoka suggested.

"These guys are playing us," Deng said.

"It wouldn't harm us if we go back to Nyan-nhialdit's hut," Aluel said.

Ochang shook his head. "It's a waste of time and energy."

"And I hope I'm not the only one feeling this rude heat," Lado said.

When I'm tired I dance
When I'm in love I'm sane
Love your friends the same
I'll be back for another chance.

"What kind of a song is that?" Ochang asked looking at Lado.

"What song?" Lado retorted back defiantly.

"The song you just sang!" Ochang said with a frown.

Lado shook his head. "I didn't sing any song. Is the heat making you crazy?"

Ochang cringed with a squint. "Okay? What's the big deal? It's just a song!"

"It's just a song, perhaps, but I said I didn't sing any song."

Nyoka! Nyoka, Nyoka!
Nyoka! Nyoka, Nyoka!

"Okay, Deng, stop singing my name!"

Deng stared curiously at Nyoka. "I didn't sing your name."

"Yes, you did...six times!" she said demonstrating with six fingers.

Confused, Deng slowly moved his eyes up the tree. His eyes met the crow's eyes. He stealthily looked at his friends one by one then at the crow. None of his friends had noticed the change on his face. He'd frowned with a vivid smile. His eyebrows were raised, his forehead creased and terrace-looking.

"Did anyone notice the crow's drawing on Umjalaba's stereo? It's..."

Deng interrupted Ochang and said slowly and quietly: "Guys, I'm going to tell you something now but don't freak out."

Lado made a crooked face. "What?"

Deng smiled satisfactorily. "Slowly look up the tree."

"Why?" Nyoka asked.

"The crow!" Ochang said and sprang up.

"He's the one who's been singing and calling Nyoka's name," Deng said.

They all sprang up and left the tree shade. The crow was still perched in the same place. His stare was cold, but frightening. The scared friends aimed their eyes at the unbecoming bird. The wild bird stood with clear majestic elegance. It was black all over except part of the abdomen and the area just below the head.

Ochang looked at Deng with doubt. "No, I don't believe you! That crow can't talk!"

"Saying a bird knows my name is freaky. It's one thing for a crow to talk and another thing for it to know my name. No, no, no!" Nyoka spoke, completely shaken.

She slowly tried to run away. The crow left the treetop and perched on the root under the mango tree. Curious and excited for the first time since the rain stopped; Deng walked slowly to the crow.

The rest started to walk away from the crow. "You're crazy, you know that?" Lado said, looking at Deng.

The crow angled his neck. "And you're delightful, Lado."

"No, he didn't just say my name?" Lado said walking back slowly.

"No, I'm going home," Nyoka said, fear in her eyes.

Ochang, Nyakong and Aluel were lost for words. They were staring with their eyes and mouths wide open.

I'm going to cry, Nyoka,
You're the most beautiful, Nyoka,
Your mum calls you Jesus's mother
I know you're kind like no other.
Listen to me Nyoka!

The crow sang as the friends stared, all lost and dumbfounded. The song was beautifully melodious.

"Are we dead?" Aluel asked.

The crow shook his head. "No, you're in denial, Aluel."

"Who's going to believe us?" Ochang said, still shaken.

"You guys now know why I didn't tell you," Deng said.

All the five friends nodded, fear and shock still in their eyes. The crow jumped down the root and the friends ran back. He shook his head and walked slowly towards Deng. Deng stood still.

"I told you to go to Nyan-nhialdit's place but you refused," the crow said.

He walked past Deng and wobbled towards the rest. Any single step by the crow was a step away by Deng's friends.

Deng turned as the crow passed him. "Wait! Wait a minute! You didn't tell us that. Umjalabla told us that," Deng said with a frown.

"Yeah, you're lying!" Nyoka said, still standing at a distance as if she was about to run.

"When will you kids listen to what I say?"

"Man, we're talking to a crow. Do you know how crazy that is?" Ochang said.

"Stop insulting me."

"I'm sorry, but you have to understand."

The crow nodded. "Lado said earlier that talking to the crow would be cool."

Lado shook his head twice. "Hey, that was just a story."

Lado was getting less fearful. He was walking slowly towards Deng and the crow.

The crow flew to an upper branch and stared at the boys and girls.

"Where are you going?" Deng asked.

"You're not listening to me so I better show you something."

"We're talking to a crow. What could be scarier than that?" Nyakong said quietly.

The crow's legs started to lengthen. The boys and girls moved back slowly as the wings flattered and started to grow.

"What's happening?" Deng said and moved back with fright. Before the legs could touch the ground, the crow slowly changed into a human being. Deng and his friends stared with their mouths wide open. The transformation ended with a familiar figure

Umjalaba?! They all said and swooned, except Deng.

"This is something!" Deng murmured.

Nyoka, Nyakong, Aluel, Lado and Ochang simultaneously woke up from the swoon.

Yaba Jada was sitting on a chair under the tree. Next to him was Nyan-nhialdit. Umjalaba was standing with Deng.

"Why didn't you tell me you were the rain-maker," Deng asked Nyan-nhialdit, smile on his face.

"There's no short-cut in life, remember that. Everything we do involves a process that needs endurance, respect and obedience. Now, to be a lawyer, a doctor, a professor, you need good grades. You kids have potential and teaching you by using mere words doesn't help with your generation. You understand with your eyes not minds. Old people are ignored or looked down upon. There is also the assumption that 'some people can't advise us.' What matters should be the message not the messenger. What should matter, indeed, is the value of the message not the beauty of the messenger; or the size of the messenger; or, for you, the tribe or race of the messenger."

The kids stared passionately and attentively as Nyan-nhialdit talked. They felt so calmed, solaced and happy; so much so, that the heat wasn't bothering them anymore. Umjalaba was now sitting on the arm of Yaba Jada's chair. The kids, including Deng, were seated on the ground in a semi-circle.

"As you grow up, many people will tell you things. You'll believe words you shouldn't believe; and you'll reject words you should believe. What I'd like to tell you is to let the love of togetherness be your *anthem*. However nice a person is, shun them if they despise others. Don't be afraid to correct, but make sure your words are meant to correct your friends with every respect they deserve. Don't despise people because they're small or because they are of different colors. Remember this. No matter what others say of your differences, you're all South Sudanese. And that's your TRIBE. Not Jieng (Dinka), not Naath (Nuer), not Bari, not Acholi, not Shilluk (collo), not Didinga and what have you. When I see the six of you, my heart is warmed and I thank God for that," Yaba Jada said. His voice was coarse but his words were endearing.

"Will it rain now?" Deng asked.

"For you to play in the rain, you mean?"

Deng smiled and said: "No, it's too hot."

"We don't need rain to be friends," Ochang said.

"Or to be happy friends," Nyakong said.

"We want to know more about how different tribes lived in the past. Can you give us a list of all old people we can talk to?" Aluel said.

"And then we can let the children in school know about our project," Deng said delightfully.

"Knowing your history is good. It's only bad if you use it against other people. We have organized a group where young people can drop in and talk to elders from different tribes. Now, it's time to go home, kids."

"Can we see the crow again?" Lado asked.

"I thought you didn't like me. Didn't you swoon when I appeared?" Umjalaba said with a hearty laugh.

"He's just naughty, but nice," Deng said. "It's time to go and play with my sister."

Umjalaba smiled, moved back a little. "Let me show you something because looks can be deceiving."

As Umjalaba moved back, his hair slowly turned white, his face wrinkled. The smooth hands turned scaly and dark. Umjalaba had turned into a grizzled woman way older than both Nyan-nhialdit and Yaba Jada. The kids sprang up, looking horrified. To make them even more horrified, the grizzled lady turned into young Nyambura.

"I told you kids. Don't despise anyone. You never know who they might turn out to be," Nyan-nhialdit said and got up.

Deng and his friends stared, completely confused and wordless.

..........Thök de Ka..........